LEO THE LOP
TAIL TWO

written by: Stephen Cosgrove
illustrated by: Robin James

A Serendipity Book

Dedicated to yesterday, today and tomor-
row...what you were, what you are, and
what you will be.

                    Stephen

In the mist of twilight wonder, when evening shadows gently glide from branch to branch, all of the creatures of the forest softly begin to fall asleep.

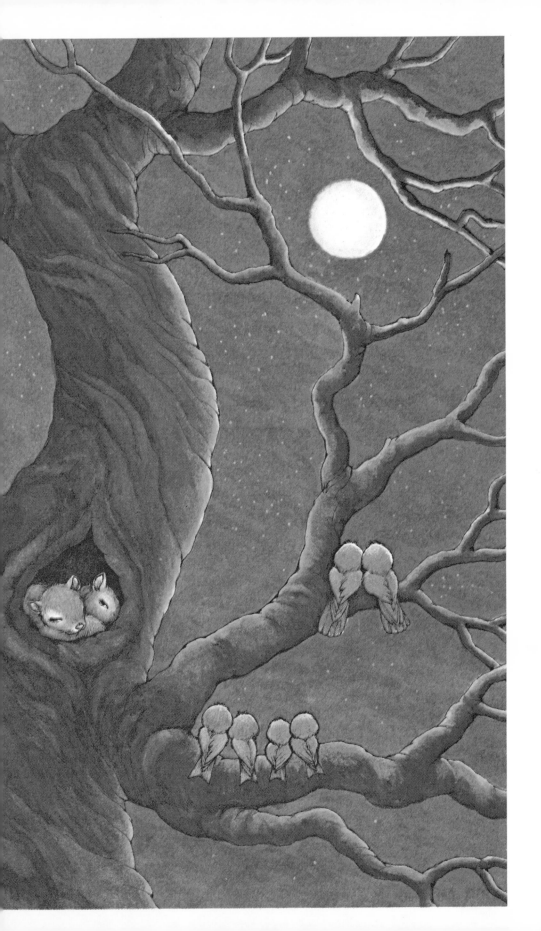

Squirrels doze, warmly wrapped in their soft, furry tails. Fawns, exhausted after frolicking in the meadows, sleep contentedly, nestled near their parents. Birds of all feathers nod gently on the branches of the trees, eyes blinking, hoping to dream of beautiful flight.

In a burrow, beneath a twisted pine, fluffy bunnies of all sorts snore and sniff quietly in their slumber.

All of the rabbits, that is, except one lop-eared rabbit called Leo, who just couldn't fall asleep. He would twitch and pitch trying desperately to fall asleep, but no matter how he tried he couldn't forget the one thing that kept him awake: he was a tiny, cute rabbit.

"Why couldn't I have been born a tough tiger?" he muttered, as he rolled over for the hundredth time. "A bad bear? A mean musk-rat? Anything but an itty bitty fluffy bunny!"

Finally, with a sob, Leo rolled over and fell into a troubled sleep.

It seemed to Leo that he had been dreaming for just a moment when, like the crash of a cymbal, the sun brought the beginning of a new day. He slowly rubbed the sleep from his eyes, yawned once, stretched twice, and finally tumbled from his soft bed of moss.

"Oh, what am I going to do?" he mumbled, as he looked into the mirror. "I don't want to be cute anymore. I want to be rough and rugged and brave!" With that he squinted his eyes, scrunched his nose, and looked just as tough as he could. Satisfied that he didn't look quite as cute, Leo brushed his teeth, and hurried off to creature school.

Leo ran just as fast as his little legs would carry him, through the twisted trail, until he reached the clearing in the wood that served as the classroom. As usual, he was just a little bit late.

As he hurried to sit down, the squirrels giggled, the little birds twittered, and all the creatures smiled because Leo was still trying to look rough, tough, and mean.

All the creatures were laughing, except the old grey owl who sat on a branch at the head of the class.

"Ahem!" muttered the old owl as he covered a smile. "Now that everyone is here we'll begin the lesson for today. I would like each of you to think of a word that best describes the way you look this morning."

All the creatures thought and thought. Then, one by one, they each stood and told the old owl the word they had thought of: "We look feathery," chirped the birds. "I look brawny," rumbled the bear. And on they went, describing how they felt in a single word. They finally came to Leo.

Leo took a deep breath, looked carefully about him and then blurted out quickly: "I look brave!"

There was a moment of silence. Then the forest glade rang with laughter. Even the owl couldn't hide his smile. "I don't see anything funny about me being brave," cried a very hurt and angry Leo.

"Well, Leo," the old owl chuckled, "perhaps fluffy or cute would have better described how you look."

Leo wiped at a furry tear as he shouted, "I don't want to be fluffy or little anymore. I want to be tough and rugged!" Once again all the creatures broke into fits of laughter. Leo stood for just a moment, tears streaming from his eyes, and then rushed into the forest.

He wandered the forest for hours and hours. "What do I have to do?" he said to himself. "Maybe if I shaved off all my fur, or lifted weights or something..."

Leo gazed into the calm waters of a stream and made ugly, tough faces, but even these couldn't make him forget the words "cute" and "fluffy." So he kept wandering farther and farther into the forest.

As the other creatures frisked about the forest glade, doing their daily chores, a wisp of smoke snaked about the boughs of a tree and climbed toward the sky. A brown squirrel sat on his haunches, sniffing at the afternoon air. "I smell smoke, but it's probably just a camp fire," he thought as he continued on his way.

By dusk, though, the wisps of smoke had turned into billowing clouds. Suddenly all around the clearing, flames shot high into the air.

All of the creatures began running about, packing up their nests, dashing here and there in absolute pandemonium. "Fire! Fire!" they shouted.

The old grey owl fluttered to the ground in the center of the glade and shouted, "Now everybody just slow down and don't panic!" The animals gathered around as the owl continued, "We must all be as calm as possible or someone will get hurt. Now, is everyone here?"

They all looked around and then someone shouted, "Yes, it looks like we're all here. All of us, that is, except that little rabbit, Leo!"

The owl thought for a moment and then said, "We'll just have to hope that he's outside the fire area. Now we must leave and move to safety."

They all looked about the clearing but the smoke was so thick that no one could see which way to go.

Leo had been moping at the far edge of the forest when he first saw the columns of smoke. "Oh no!" he said, "That fire looks like it's burning right in the middle of the clearing where I live." He wondered for a moment about what he should do, then rushed off towards the fire.

He ran and ran until he ran out of breath and then he ran some more. Finally he reached the edge of the smoke and flames that enclosed the clearing where he lived. To his dismay he could find none of his friends. "Oh dear!" he thought, "They must be trapped inside."

Without a second thought for his own safety he crouched real low to the ground and began to follow the path into the clearing, through the thick grey smoke.

Leo finally reached the center of the clearing where all the creatures were searching for a way out of the inferno. "Quickly," shouted Leo. "Everybody hold hands and follow me."

Leo looked so sure of himself and so unafraid that everyone followed him without question and they were led carefully through the heavy smoke and towards safety.

Finally they reached the safety of a hill on the far side of the forest, away from the fire. All the animals gathered around Leo, cheering and shouting.

"Well," said the owl, "I certainly was wrong about you and your chosen word. For today you were certainly brave."

"No," said Leo blushing deeply, "if it had not been for the fact that I was small, I would never have been low enough to the ground to see the trail into the clearing. I guess being cute and furry doesn't mean you can't be brave." With that the other animals cheered Leo the brave and Leo the lion-hearted and continued their cheering far into the night.

SO IF YOU'RE CUTE AND FURRY,
OR EVEN IF YOU'RE NOT,
REMEMBER LEO THE LION HEARTED
AND THE LESSON THAT HE GOT.